D0575875

To our family: Let's go to the beach! —LMK & KHM

PHILOMEL BOOKS

An imprint of Penguin Random House LLC, New York

First published in the United States of America by Philomel,
an imprint of Penguin Random House LLC, 2021.

Text copyright © 2021 by Laura McGee Kvasnosky.

Illustrations copyright © 2021 by Laura McGee Kvasnosky and Kate Harvey McGee.

Penguin supports copyright. Copyright fuels creativity, encourages diverse voices, promotes free speech, and creates a vibrant culture. Thank you for buying an authorized edition of this book and for complying with copyright laws by not reproducing, scanning, or distributing any part of it in any form without permission. You are supporting writers and allowing Penguin to continue to publish books for every reader.

Philomel Books is a registered trademark of Penguin Random House LLC.

Visit us online at penguinrandomhouse.com

Library of Congress Cataloging-in-Publication Data is available.

Manufactured in China

ISBN 9780593118016

10 9 8 7 6 5 4 3 2 1

Edited by Talia Benamy.

Design by Monique Sterling.
Text set in Adderville.

With thanks to marine science teacher Susan Barth.

Kvasnosky, Laura McGee,
Ocean lullaby /
2021.
33305251765180
sa   07/15/21

an Lullaby

Laura McGee Kvasnosky

Kate Harvey McGee

PHILOMEL BOOKS

Song floats up, moon smiles down,
while we rock to ocean sounds.

Shhh, hush. Shhh, hush. The ocean's soothing song.

Shhh, hush. Shhh, hush. We can sing along.

Far offshore the big whales doze.
Moms nudge calves to keep them close.

Turtles float and shut their eyes.
Jellies undulate and rise.

Shhh, hush. Shhh, hush. The ocean's soothing song.

Dolphins drift and mantas glide
through the rocking, rolling tide.

Along the reef, fish hide and spread,
tucked into their coral bed.

Shhh, hush. Shhh, hush. We can sing along.

Octopus dreams in her cave
underneath the swelling waves.

Tide pools catch the moonlight's glow.
Stars above, sea stars below.

Shhh, hush. Shhh, hush. The ocean's soothing song.

Monk seals find a sandy shore,
stretch their flippers, start to snore.

Rising waves break, spill and reach,
smoothing footsteps from the beach.

Shhh, hush. Shhh, hush. We can sing along.

You, my sweet, my sleepy child,
rest here in my arms awhile.
As the new moon rides the sky,
dream the ocean lullaby.

Shhh, *hush.* Shhh, *hush.*

Shhhhhh . . .